DISNEY·PIXAR

TOY STORY 3

Best Friends
Magnetic Buddy Storybook

adapted by Chip Lovitt
illustrated by Caroline Egan,
Adrienne Brown, Scott Tilley, and
Studio IBOIX

Reader's
Digest
Children's Books®

Pleasantville, New York • Montréal, Québec • Bath, United Kingdom

Woody the cowboy, space ranger Buzz Lightyear, and the rest of Andy's toys had had many wonderful playtime adventures with Andy over the years. But now, it looked like the good times were coming to an end. Andy had grown up and was leaving for college soon. It was time to leave his childhood toys behind.

The toys were worried. They had survived countless yard sales and giveaways, but this was different. What would happen to them after Andy left? "We're getting thrown away!" Rex exclaimed.

But Woody reassured his friends. "We're not getting thrown away! You wait—Andy's going to tuck us in the attic. It'll be safe and warm."

"And we'll be together," Buzz added.

Place Woody into the picture so he can reassure his friends.

Later that afternoon, Andy started to pack for college. Andy's mom came into his room with trash bags and boxes. "Anything you're not taking to college either goes into the attic or the trash," she said. Andy grabbed a trash bag and threw the toys in—except for Woody. Andy put Woody into a box marked "College." He left the trash bag in the hallway, planning to put it in the attic, but he got distracted. Andy's mom, thinking it was trash, picked it up, and took it to the curb. Woody raced outside to help his friends.

As the toys huddled fearfully in the trash bag, they heard a garbage truck approaching. The toys had to act quickly. Using Rex's pointy tail, they punched a hole in the garbage bag and fled to the garage.

Woody raced across the driveway and into the garage. He tried once again to convince the other toys that Andy truly meant to keep them, and that their place was in Andy's attic.

The toys didn't believe Woody, so they hatched a plan. They jumped into a box of toys in Andy's mom's car. The box was being donated to Sunnyside Daycare. Woody tried to push his friends out of the car, but Andy's mom slammed the hatchback shut, trapping Woody with the other toys.

**Place Woody into the picture
so he can help his friends.**

When they got to the daycare center, the toys saw lots of happy children playing with all kinds of toys. The daycare center looked like a dream come true.

A big pink teddy bear walked up to greet Andy's toys. "Well, hello there. Welcome to Sunnyside," the bear said. "I'm Lots-o'-Huggin' Bear. You can call me Lotso." Lotso was the leader at Sunnyside. He showed Andy's toys the room where they would be staying.

Woody tried to convince his friends to go back to Andy's. But none of the toys wanted to return with Woody—not even Buzz. "So this is it," Woody said as he left his friends.

Place Woody into the picture so he can greet Lotso.

Woody was determined to make it back to Andy's house. He escaped out of a bathroom window and made his way to the roof, where he found an old kite. Clutching the kite, he sailed off the roof. Unfortunately, the kite broke and Woody ended up stuck in a tree. Bonnie, a little girl from the daycare center, found Woody hanging from the tree branch and took him home.

Inside the daycare center, the toys quickly learned that their dream come true was really a nightmare. They were assigned to the Caterpillar Room, where shrieking toddlers chewed, slobbered over, and played roughly with the toys. One toddler even used Buzz's head as a hammer! Andy's toys knew they had to get out of the Caterpillar Room.

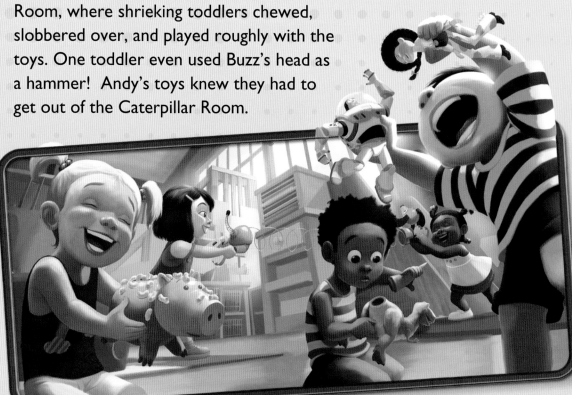

Place Woody into the picture so Bonnie can rescue him.

Meanwhile at Bonnie's house, Woody met all of Bonnie's toys. Bonnie was a lively girl with a big imagination. Together the toys had an amazing playtime. Woody hadn't had so much fun in years. But when some of Bonnie's toys told him what a bully Lotso was, Woody realized his friends needed help. He would have to go back to Sunnyside.

Place Woody into the picture so he can talk to Bonnie's toys.

So the next morning, Woody stowed away in Bonnie's backpack when she went to Sunnyside Daycare. Woody made his way to the Caterpillar Room. When the toddlers went out to the playground for recess, Woody came out of hiding.

"Psst! Psst! Hey guys!" he whispered. His friends were surprised but very happy to see him. "From now on, we stick together," Woody told them. "We're busting out of here tonight."

"There's no way out of here," Rex protested.

But Woody had figured out a way to escape. "There is one way out," he said, pointing to the trash chute.

Place Woody into the picture
so he can help plan the toys' escape.

But getting out of the daycare center would be no easy task. Lotso had several toys from his gang patrolling the hallways. That night, the toys made a daring escape from the Caterpillar Room and made their way outside. Just before dawn, the toys slipped down the trash chute in the wall that surrounded the daycare center. But instead of finding freedom, the toys found themselves face to face with Lotso and and his bullying friends. Lotso wouldn't let Andy's toys go.

Just then a garbage truck drove up. It hoisted the Dumpster up and dumped all its contents—including Andy's toys—into the back of the truck. The next thing the toys knew, they were dumped at a landfill.

Place Woody into the picture so he can walk across Slinky Dog to confront Lotso.

Moments later, a bulldozer began pushing the piles of garbage. The toys found themselves trapped in a churning tide of trash. They landed on a conveyor belt full of garbage. To the toys' horror, they could see they were headed right for a massive shredding machine.

Suddenly Slinky Dog flew into the air and ended up stuck to a conveyor belt high above the other toys. The belt was magnetized, and thanks to the metal in Slinky's spring, he had been pulled up to safety. Woody and the others quickly grabbed metal objects and they, too, were pulled up in the nick of time.

Moments later, the toys dropped down to another conveyor belt. They thought it would lead to safety. Instead, it led right to a fiery incinerator. The toys could feel the intense heat from the furnace.

Place Woody into the picture so he can be pulled to safety.

Just when it seemed the toys were destined for a fiery fate in the incinerator, a giant claw dropped down and snatched them up. The Aliens had commandeered a crane and pulled their friends out of danger's way. The Aliens steered the crane away from the incinerator and lowered the toys to the ground.

The toys noticed a garbage truck was about the leave the landfill so they jumped aboard. A short time later they found themselves safely back at Andy's house.

They slipped through an open window and made their way back to Andy's room. Woody turned to his old pal, Buzz, and shook hands. "This isn't goodbye," Woody said. "I know we'll see each other again."

"You know where to find us, cowboy," Buzz said. He and the other toys climbed into a box marked "Attic." Woody climbed into the "College" box.

While he was waiting, Woody looked up and saw a picture of Andy with all his toys. Suddenly he knew what he had to do. He slipped out of his box, wrote something on a sticky note, and stuck it on the "Attic" box.

Attic

Place Woody into the picture so he can say goodbye to his friends.

When Andy came to pick up the last of the boxes, he saw the sticky note. It had the words "Donate to: Bonnie Anderson, 1225 Sycamore" written on it. He opened the box and was amazed to see all the toys he thought had been thrown out. "Hey, Mom," he called out. "Do you really think I should donate these toys?"

"It's up to you, honey," she replied. "Whatever you want to do."

So Andy drove to Bonnie's house where he found the little girl playing in her yard.